Mr Bear to the Rescue

Debi Gliori

ORCHARD BOOKS

for all those Mr Bears:
Guri and Kari, Gay and Michael,
Ben, Sophie and Patrick,
my very dear Kirsty,
Belinda and Lyndsay
Jaca and Judy
but most of all
for you.
You.

ORCHARD BOOKS
96 Leonard Street, London EC2A 4RH
Orchard Books Australia
14 Mars Road, Lane Cove, NSW 2066
ISBN 1 86039 474 4 (paperback)
ISBN 1 85213 983 8 (hardback)
First published in Great Britain 1996
First paperback publication 1997
Copyright © Debi Gliori 1996
The right of Debi Gliori to be identified as the author of this
work has been asserted by her in accordance with the
Copyright, Designs and Patents Act, 1988.
A CIP catalogue record for this book is available from the
British Library.
Printed in Singapore

It was a wild and windy night in the forest.

The kind of night where the best place to be was in bed, snug and warm, with windows and doors tightly shut to keep the weather out.

Mr Bear was tucked up in bed,
while outside the wind was
shaking the windows and
howling down the chimney,
trying to get in.

"What was that noise?"
said Mrs Bear, sitting up.

"Just the wind, dear,"
said Mr Bear.

"I thought I heard a voice
calling *Help!*" said Mrs Bear.

"Help!" said a small voice.

"There," said Mrs Bear.
"I did hear a voice. Go and
see who it is, dear?"

Mr Bear obediently went downstairs.
As he opened the front door,
a blast of wind blew out his candle
and peppered him with fallen leaves.

"Please help," said a very small voice
from somewhere around Mr Bear's ankles.

Clinging on to Mr Bear's doorstep
was Mr Rabbit-Bunn.

"Our warren has collapsed," he wailed.
"The Hoot-Toowits' nest has blown away,
the Buzzes' hive is ruined and I have
to go back because we can't find baby
Flora *anywhere*," and Mr Rabbit-Bunn
ran off into the night.

"Help is on its way," said Mr Bear, lighting
a lantern, packing tools and grabbing a honey
sandwich, just in case.

"Do be careful, dear," called Mrs Bear, as
Mr Bear was blown down the garden path.

"Don't worry," said Mr Bear, feeling very
worried indeed. "I'll be fine."

It was a long way to the Rabbit-Bunns' house.
Mr Bear tripped and stumbled over fallen branches
and several times his lantern nearly blew out.

"I wish I was back in my warm bed," thought Mr Bear.
Icy rain blew into Mr Bear's face as he struggled uphill.
"Just a little further," said Mr Bear to encourage himself.

A tangle of feathers and claws blew into
Mr Bear's face. "Aaaaargh!" he shrieked.
"Eeeek!" squawked Mr Hoot-Toowit.
"Oh, it's *you*!" they both cried in unison.
Mr Bear struggled to his feet
and peered into the darkness.

"I can't see your house
anywhere," he said.
"You're standing in it,"
said Mr Hoot-Toowit sadly.
"Goodness, so I am," said Mr Bear.
There, all around, lay the battered remains
of the tree that Mr Hoot-Toowit had shared
with his family, the Buzz family and the Rabbit-Bunns.

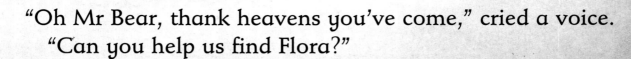

"Oh Mr Bear, thank heavens you've come," cried a voice.
   "Can you help us find Flora?"
   "And can you fix our hive?"
   "And mend our nest?"

Mr Bear was instantly surrounded
by rabbits and owls and bees,
all beseeching him for help.
"Help," thought Mr Bear,
"What on earth am I supposed to do?"
He scrabbled around in his tool kit
and found the honey sandwich that
he'd thrown in there as he left his house.

A brilliant idea occurred to him.

"What's that for?" asked one of the small Rabbit-Bunns.

"Glue," said Mr Bear, peeling the sandwich apart. "Hive-glue, in fact. Look, I'll spread a little bit here and another dollop there and . . ."

"End up with a sticky mess," groaned a small Buzz.

"Oh dear," said Mr Bear, "let's take the hive home for Mrs Bear to fix. She's very good at that sort of thing."

"What about my nest?" said Mr Hoot-Toowit.
"I'll just have a look," said Mr Bear, picking it up.

The nest fell apart in his paws. Mrs Hoot-Toowit sighed.
"Ah," said Mr Bear, "Mrs Bear'll knit you another
in no time."

As the animals put the sticky hive and broken nest into Mr Bear's toolkit, the heavens opened.

Rain poured down through the trees, seeking out anything that was dry and turning it instantly cold and soggy. The animals ran for shelter.

Mr Bear's lantern hissed, fizzled and went out.
  "How will we ever find Flora now?"
wailed Mrs Rabbit-Bunn.
  Mr Bear looked up at the sky anxiously.
  "Good grief," he said.
  "What's that?" said Mr Hoot-Toowit
through a mouthful of twigs.

"I've found Flora!" yelled Mr Bear pointing upwards. There, high in the branches of the sheltering tree, was a small rabbit, still wrapped in a blanket and fast asleep.

"I'll just climb up there
and get her," said Mr Bear.
    "What a hero you are,"
sighed Mrs Rabbit-Bunn.
    Mr Bear didn't feel heroic
as he inched up the tree.

The slippy rain-soaked branches
gave out alarming groans and creaks
as he grabbed them.

Mr Bear disentangled the blanket
from the branch, cradled Flora in his
arms and . . .

"Aaaargh!" yelled Mr Bear.
   "Wheeeeee," said Flora,
waking up.
   "Gosh, what a good idea,"
said Mr Rabbit-Bunn,
as Flora's blanket fanned
out into a perfect parachute,
and Mr Bear and the bunny
floated safely to the ground.

"What a brilliant Mr Bear!" said Mrs Rabbit-Bunn,
hugging Mr Bear's knees.

"Let's get these children tucked up in bed,"
said Mr Bear, loading the Rabbit-Bunns,
Buzzes and Hoot-Toowits into his toolkit.

"It's very dark," said Mr Hoot-Toowit.

"I can't see," wailed a small Rabbit-Bunn.

"Neither can I," thought Mr Bear, pushing his laden toolkit to the top of a hill. But there, off in the distance, was his house with all the lights on, shining through the darkness.

"Hold on tight," he said. "We're nearly home."

And much later, when towels and blankets
had been found for everyone, and Mrs Bear's
hot nettle soup had warmed every tummy, large
and small, the bear house filled with snores
from the Buzzes, the Hoot-Toowits and
the Rabbit-Bunns.

Baby Bear clambered up Mr Bear's leg.
Mr Bear sank into a chair with a groan.

Mrs Bear looked up from her nest-knitting
with a mischievous smile.

"What a brilliant Mr Bear your daddy is,"
she said. "So good at fixing things."

Mr Bear gave a huge yawn.

"In fact," continued Mrs Bear,
"there's a few things round here that could
do with being fixed by that daddy. There's the
squeaky bathroom door, the blocked sink
and the smoky chimney…"

Mr Bear gave a loud snore.

"...but they can all wait till tomorrow,"
said Mrs Bear, fetching a warm blanket for
Mr Bear and Baby Bear. "Even brilliant Mr Bears
need to be tucked in at times," she said, as she
blew out the candles and headed upstairs to bed.